Does This Make Me Beautiful?

Written by Harriet Morse
Illustrations by Megan D. Wellman

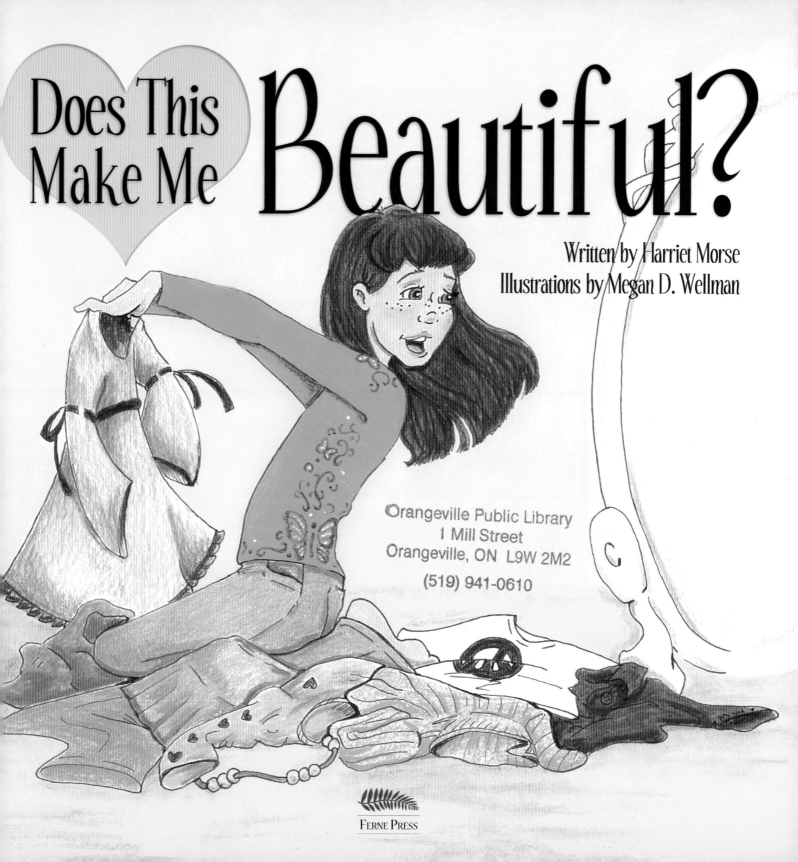

FERNE PRESS

Does This Make Me Beautiful?
Copyright © 2011 by Harriet Morse
Illustrations by Megan D. Wellman
Layout and cover design by Kimberly Franzen
Illustrations created with colored pencils and ink
Printed in the United States of America

Summary: A young girl discovers that true beauty doesn't come from clothes or accessories.

Library of Congress Cataloging-in-Publication Data
Morse, Harriet
Does This Make Me Beautiful?/Harriet Morse – First Edition
ISBN-13: 978-1-933916-73-6
  1. Juvenile Fiction. 2. Self-esteem. 3. Self-confidence.
I. Morse, Harriet II. Does This Make Me Beautiful?
Library of Congress Control Number: 2010933836

FERNE PRESS

Ferne Press is an imprint of Nelson Publishing & Marketing
366 Welch Road, Northville, MI 48167
www.nelsonpublishingandmarketing.com
(248) 735-0418

Thank you to my oldest daughter, Jillian, who continually teaches me that it doesn't matter what you wear as long as it is comfortable and you live through your heart.

Thank you to my middle daughter, Ella, whose *bountiful* spirit inspires me everyday to keep my own spirit shining.

Thank you to my youngest daughter, Lexie, who shares her love so freely.

I also want to thank my husband, Michael, who always believed I could publish this *book* and live my dreams.

"Mom, guess what? Caitlyn asked me to play! You know, that popular girl down the street. Can you believe it? I'm at her house. Can I stay? Please?" I blurt out.

"Sure, Harriet, that's great! You've always wanted to play with her. Have fun! Just be home for dinner," my mom says. "I can stay!" I scream. "Can I see your room?"

"Yeah, my room rocks," Caitlyn says.
"Wow! Your room is so cool. You have posters of every girl on TV.
It's incredible! Where'd you get all of these posters?" I ask.

"My mom bought them for me. She knows I love them. Everyone does! Aren't they beautiful? Their hair is always shiny, and their clothes always look perfect," Caitlyn says. "Don't I look just like her?"

"You really do." Maybe that's why *she's so popular*, I wonder. "Do I look like any of them?" I ask, wishing I do.

"No, you have red hair and a ton of freckles," Caitlyn says.
"But it's okay, Harriet, you're nice."
Who wants to be nice? I think. I want to be beautiful, just like
Caitlyn and those girls in her posters.

"I have a great idea! Let's dress like one of them for school tomorrow," Caitlyn says. "It'll be fun. Here, take one of my posters so you know what to wear. I'm sure you can find something to... kind of make you look like her. I already know what I'm going to wear," Caitlyn brags.

"Thanks!" I say, having no idea what to wear, but determined to find something good.

I couldn't sleep all night thinking about what Caitlyn said. But maybe she won't even notice my red hair and freckles if I'm wearing the perfect outfit. Let's see. I have lots of skirts, shirts, belts with all kinds of dangling charms, and fancy dresses. What will make me as beautiful as she is?

"Mom, I need your help!" I shout. "What can I wear to look just like her? I promised Caitlyn I would find something. Isn't she beautiful? Caitlyn thinks I'm nice, but not beautiful. I want to be beautiful!" I tell my mom, barely taking a breath.

"Slow down. Where did you get this poster?" "Caitlyn gave it to me. She has a ton of them, all my favorite girls on TV. She looks just like the blond girl on that dance show. That's why I want to look like this girl, minus my ugly hair and freckles."

"Wait a minute, you're beautiful inside and out. You're sweet, loving, and you care about doing the right thing. And your red hair and freckles make you who you are. Wouldn't it be boring if we all looked alike? Think of a snowflake. There are no two exactly the same. They are all beautiful, and so are we. Come with me."

"When I was your age, I didn't understand what true beauty was either. I got lost in trying to look and act exactly like my best friend. Then Grandma Ruby gave me a very special mirror. It helped me see myself more clearly, and it will help you, too. Now it's time I pass it down to you."

"You're giving me that big mirror from your bedroom? It's amazing. I always thought the decoration on top looked just like eyes."

Not answering me, my mom says, "Take a good look in this mirror. You may have never really seen yourself in it. Now, please get dressed, honey, while I move this into your room."

"I still wish I were beautiful. And I could never let Caitlyn down. I'm lucky to be her friend."

I reach for my favorite outfit, skip right up to the mirror, and ask, "Does this make me beautiful?"

Suddenly what I thought was decoration on top of the mirror shakes "No" from side to side.
"Did the mirror move? Are those really eyes? Did they say no?"
Gasping for breath, I look at myself again and think, *Maybe the mirror's right, even though I've tried on all of these clothes.*

Somewhere in here I know I have a skirt just like hers. I pull clothes off my shelves. "Here it is. Okay, this top will work."
I walk right back to the mirror and ask, "Does this make me beautiful?"
Again the mirror's eyes shake "No."

"My fanciest dress has to work. It's kind of funky. Does this make me beautiful?"

But the mirror's eyes still shake "No."

"This is so frustrating! I bet Caitlyn's already dressed! Okay, let me think. I've got it! I forgot my gold necklace. Now! Does *this* make me beautiful?"

Immediately the mirror says, "No."

"Darn it," I groan.

I pull off my dress and necklace and stand there face to face with only myself and yell, "Ahhh!"

After a minute, I hear a voice from within. It says, "Look again."
I slowly lift my head and what I see I can hardly believe. What's happening? My heart is beaming so bright that I can actually see it shine.

I feel my heartbeat with the palms of my hands. Each beat gives me goose bumps and makes me proud to be who I am.

"Mom, come here! Even my red hair and freckles look great!" I shout.

Then, for the first time, the mirror's eyes shake up and down, over and over again.

"That's right, honey. True beauty comes from the inside and shines through you, just like you see in the mirror. It has nothing to do with what you wear or the color of your hair. I'm so proud of you. I know your Grandma Ruby would be, too."

"What'll I tell Caitlyn?"

"Tell her the truth; it feels really good to be yourself. You'll see, feeling good about yourself is often contagious. Who knows, maybe Caitlyn will see your joy and even want to try herself on one day."

"I don't know about that, Mom, but I know I'm the only one I want to be."

"I love you, Harriet."

"I love you, too, Mom."

"You have to hurry, you don't want to be late," my mom says.
I quickly grab a plain T-shirt and an old pair of jeans.
I know exactly what I want to wear today. My heart!
"Okay, Mom. I'm ready for school!" I sing.

Inner beauty is a notion I have tried on and taken off regularly. It's something I have struggled with since I was a child. I truly believed that how you looked and what you wore determined how beautiful you were. Now as a mother of three girls, I do my best to teach by example, loving myself from the inside out.

This story came to me one morning after my three-year-old daughter asked me if her dress made her beautiful. My stomach dropped. At that moment, I knew I could not turn back. I had to do everything possible to teach my daughter to love herself fully. That day this book was born.

I hope this story inspires children to let their hearts shine and feel proud of who they are, no matter what they are wearing.

~Harriet Morse

Harriet Morse has spent the last twelve years growing herself and studying life. What she has learned continues to help her every day. Harriet is married to a loving man named Michael, and they have three amazing girls: Jillian, Ella, and Lexie. Harriet and her family live in Huntington Woods and Chelsea, Michigan. To learn more about Harriet, please visit www.doesthismakemebeautiful.com.

Megan D. Wellman grew up in Redford, Michigan, and currently resides with her husband, Brent, daughter, Kylee, two Great Danes, and a cat in Canton, Michigan. She holds a bachelor's degree in fine arts from Eastern Michigan University with a minor in children's theater. *Does This Make Me Beautiful?* is Megan's ninth book. Her books include *Liam's Luck and Finnegan's Fortune*, *King of Dilly Dally*, *This Babe So Small*, *Lonely Teddy*, *Grandma's Ready*, *...and that is why we teach*, *Being Bella*, and *Read to Me, Daddy!* which are all available from Ferne Press.